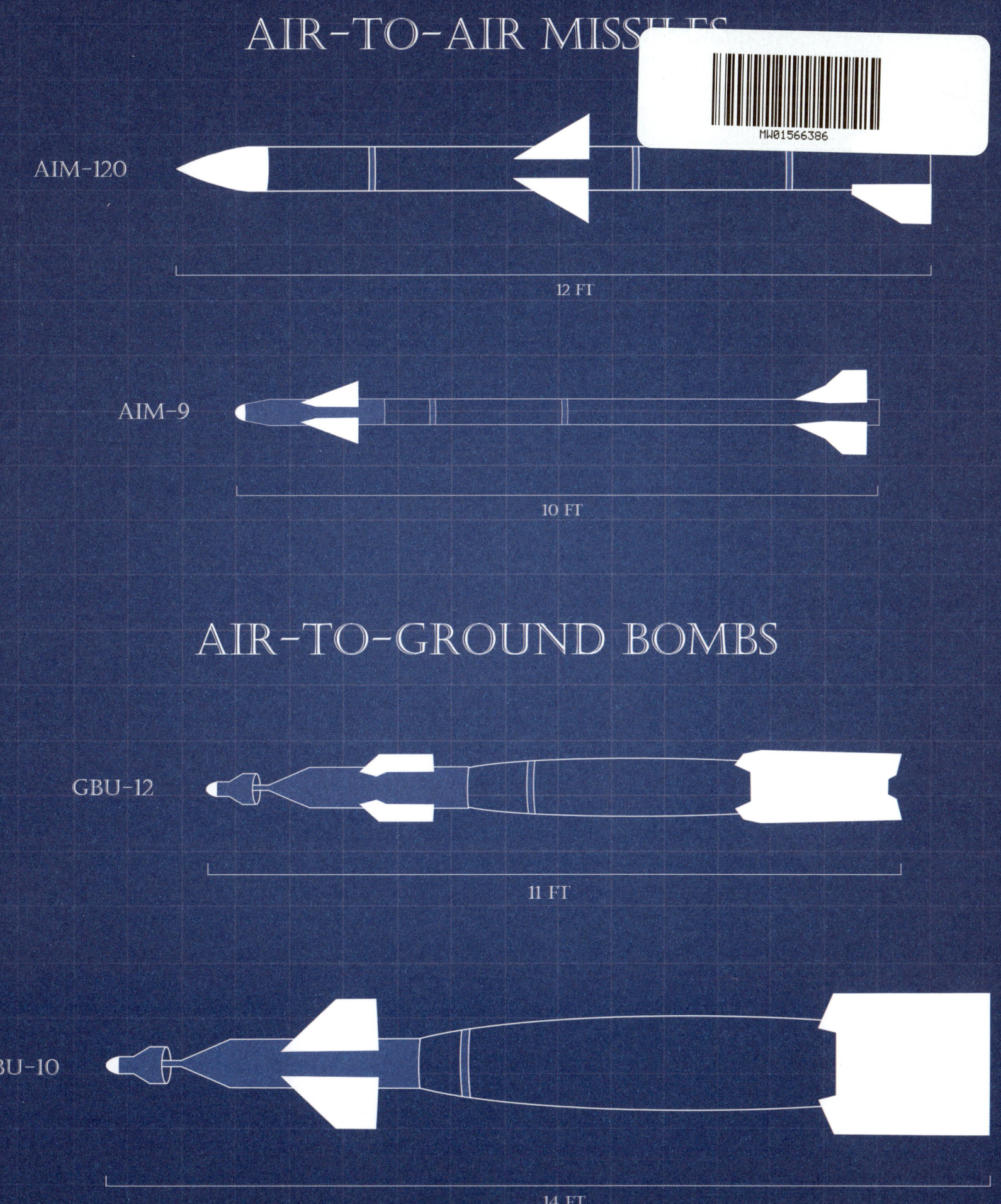

Sharks of the Sky

A Fighter Pilot's Jet Flight

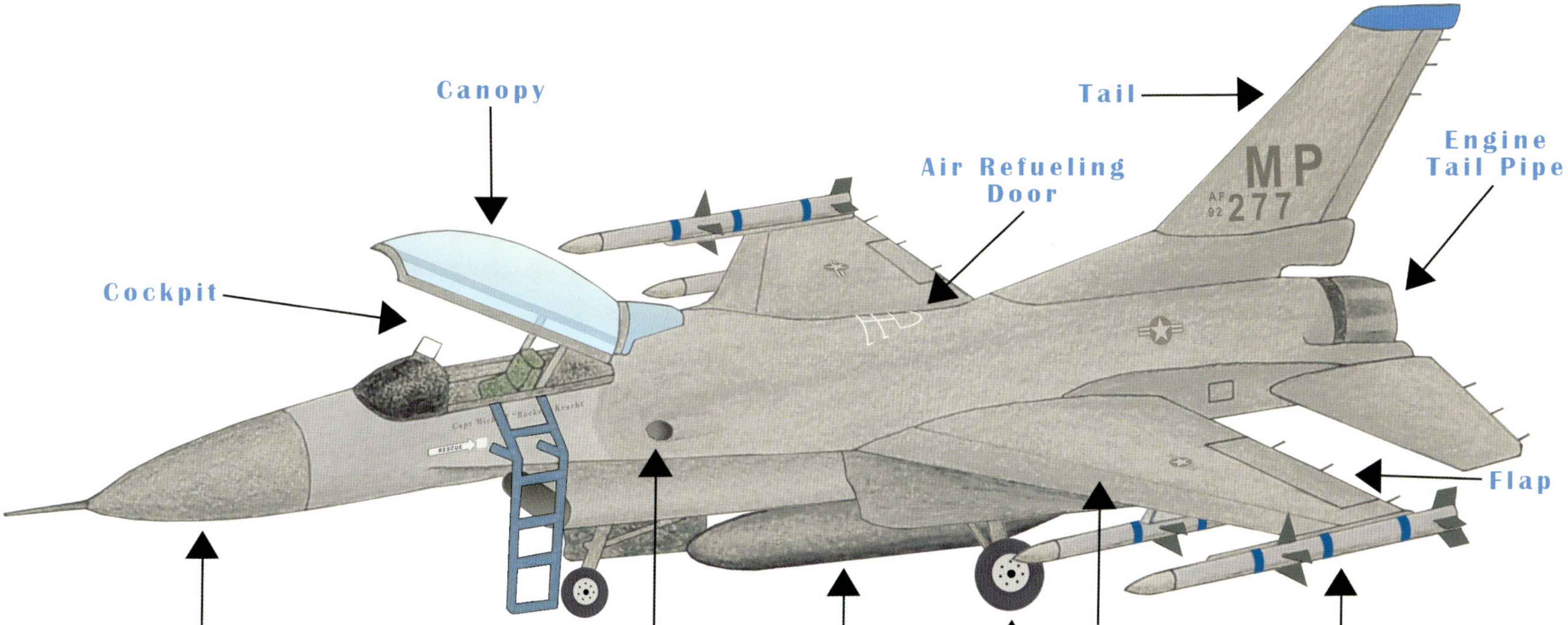

Canopy

Tail

Air Refueling Door

Engine Tail Pipe

Cockpit

Flap

Nose Cone

Gun (20mm)

Wing

Missile

Landing Gear

External Gas Tank

Written and illustrated by

Michael Kracht

Majella Publishing

Welcome to Fighter Country, USA

Sharks of the Sky: A Fighter Pilot's Jet Flight

Text and illustrations copyright © 2018 by Michael Kracht

All rights reserved. No part of this book may be reproduced or transmitted in any form or by any means, electronic or mechanical, including photocopying, recording, or by any information storage retrieval system, without written permission from the author.

First published in the United States of America in 2018 by Majella Publishing LLC

First Edition

Printed and bound in China

Library of Congress Control Number: 2017912069

ISBN: 978-0-692-93174-5

A special thanks to my wife: Thank you for all the support, love, and patience. You ultimately allowed this book to come to fruition.

10 9 8 7 6 5 4 3 2 1

Humbly dedicated to the men and women who have given their lives for this country.

The Missing Man Formation

Flight Map

Early in the morning, fighter pilots begin their day preparing and planning for the flight that awaits them. Today's flight will consist of two F-16s—supersonic fighter jets capable of carrying missiles and bombs, each flown by a single pilot.

The jets have been given call signs for identification purposes. "Shark 1" and "Shark 2" will take off at 0800 ("zero eight hundred"), practice dogfighting over the Appalachian Mountains of North Carolina, air-to-air refuel high above the Atlantic Ocean, and then return to base.

The time is now 0700, and the fighter pilots head out to their mighty "Vipers" (a nickname for F-16s). Shark 1 has tail number 907, and Shark 2 has tail number 277. The pilots begin their pre-flight checks of the F-16s by walking around the aircraft, tapping the tires, and carefully looking over each part of the plane. Then, the pilots climb the ladders, squeeze into the cockpits, fasten their seatbelts and harnesses, and, finally, close the jets' canopies.

Legend

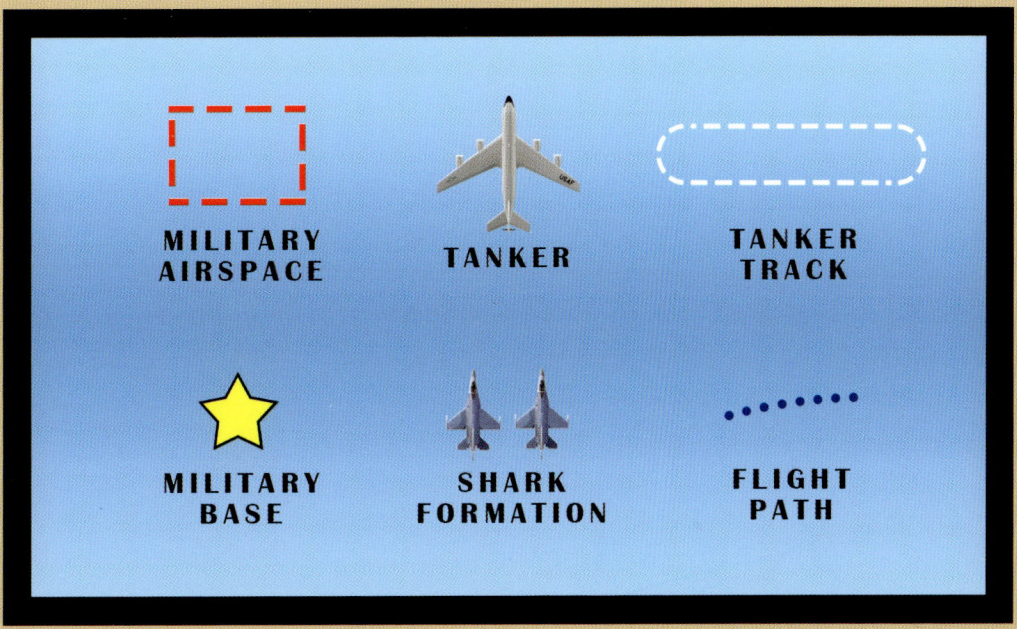

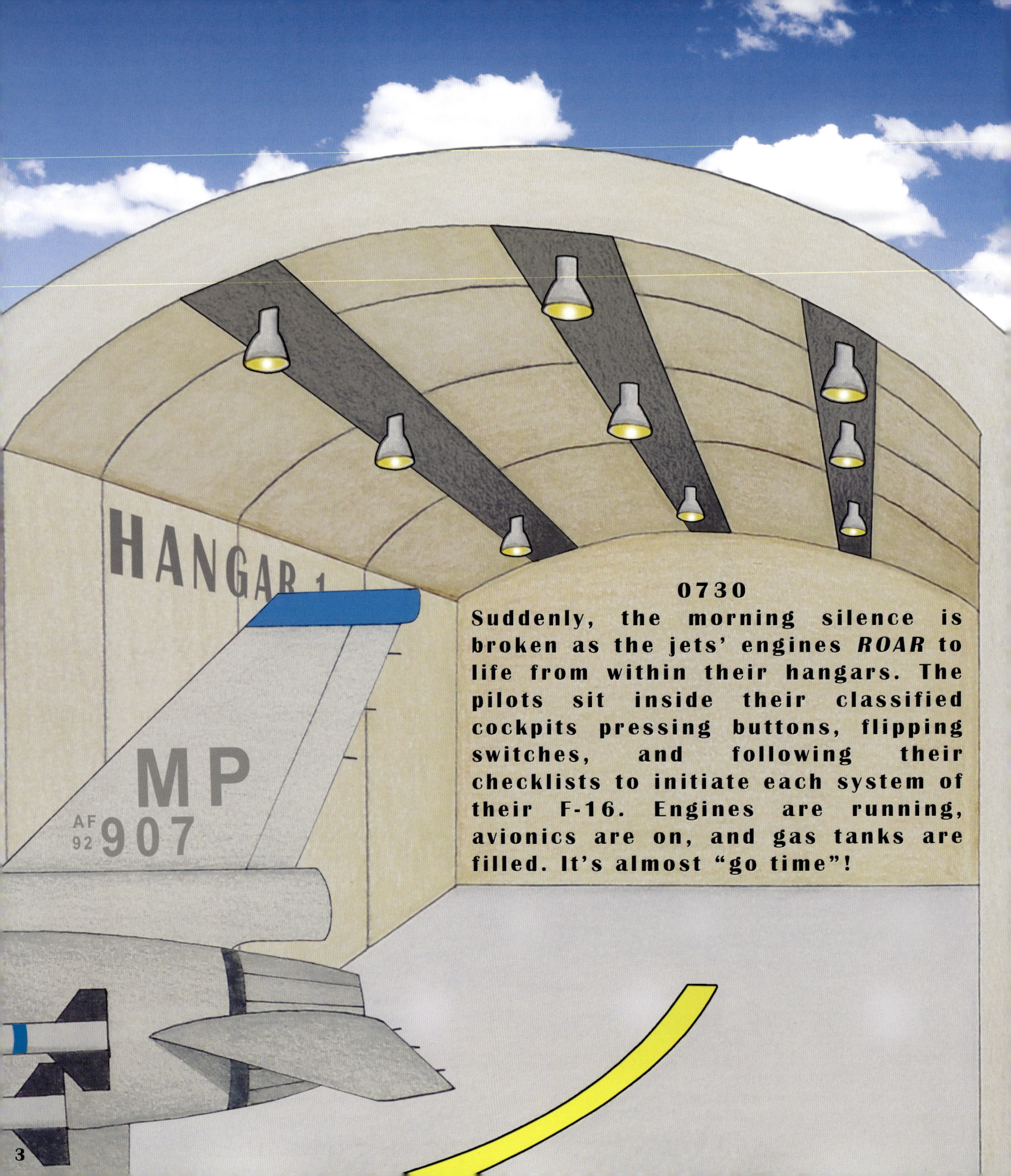

0730
Suddenly, the morning silence is broken as the jets' engines *ROAR* to life from within their hangars. The pilots sit inside their classified cockpits pressing buttons, flipping switches, and following their checklists to initiate each system of their F-16. Engines are running, avionics are on, and gas tanks are filled. It's almost "go time"!

0740

The pilots' hearts pound with excitement as they taxi out to Runway 36. Their planned takeoff time is now just a few minutes away. Shark 1 will be the flight lead, and Shark 2 will be the wingman in this two-ship formation.

Pre-takeoff checklists are checked and checked again.

Flight controls: *Operating.*
Fuel flow: *Normal.*
Ejection seat: *Armed and ready.*

Shark 1 and Shark 2 are now ready for takeoff!

0800
Shark 1 pushes the throttle forward into the maximum thrust position and barrels down the runway. The thundering rumble of the shooting fuel and flame in the engine's afterburner is heard and felt for miles around. Fifteen seconds later, Shark 2 follows behind. The much-anticipated flight is under way...

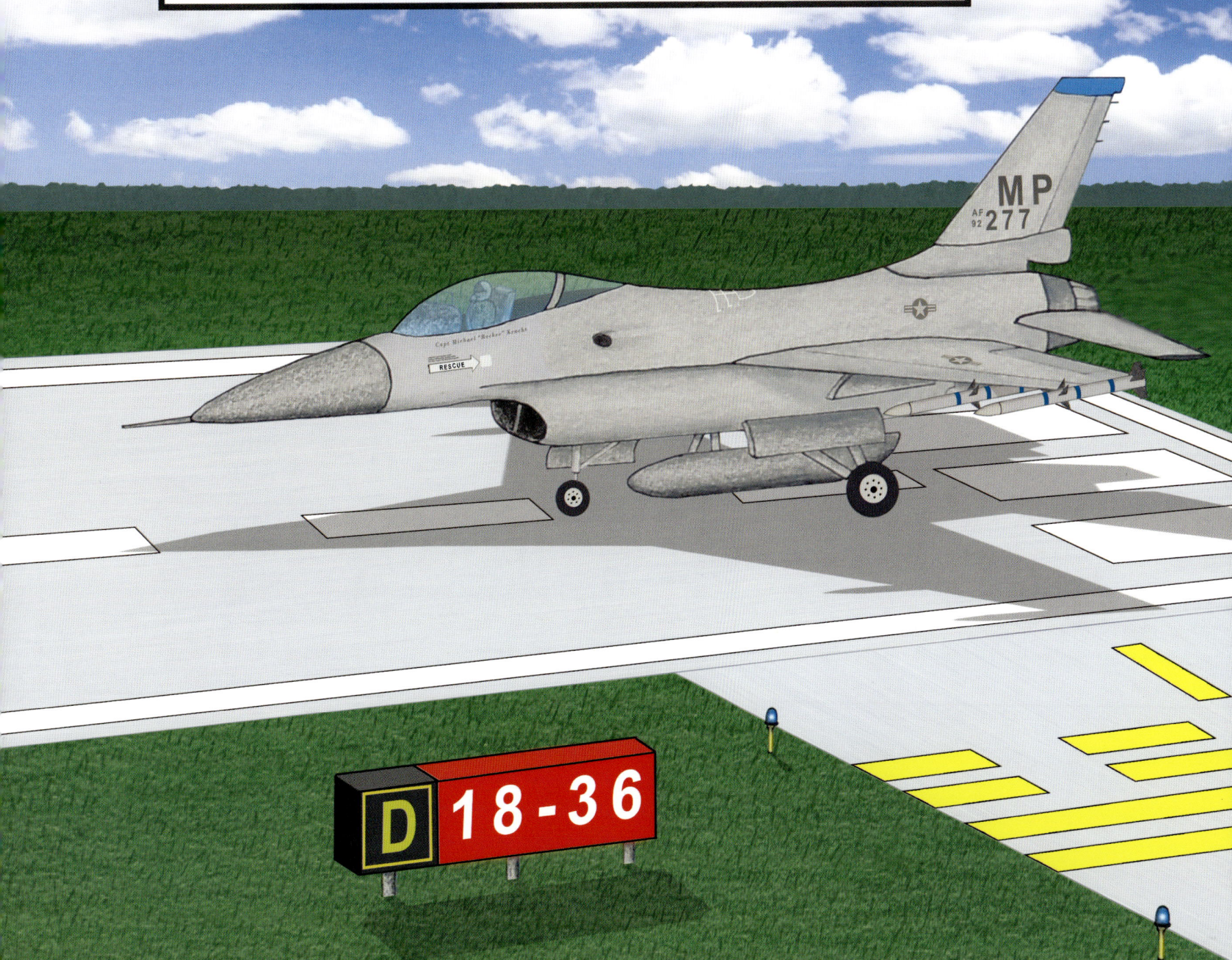

0801
The runway almost immediately disappears, and the ground begins to blur beneath Shark Formation as they power away from Planet Earth. The fighter jets continue to accelerate faster and faster, passing speeds greater than 300 miles per hour! Although the two jets took off just 15 seconds apart, Shark 1 is now more than a mile ahead of Shark 2. Shark 2 must catch up: Gear up, flaps up, time to "turn and burn!" as the fighter pilots say.

0815

Until now, each fighter pilot has been so focused on taking off safely that there has been no time for communicating over the radio. Radio silence is finally broken as Shark 1 calls to the wingman, "Don't lose sight of me back there. We have some thick clouds ahead, and it might get a bit bumpy."

"Bring on those white puffies!" responds Shark 2, ready for some extreme maneuvering.

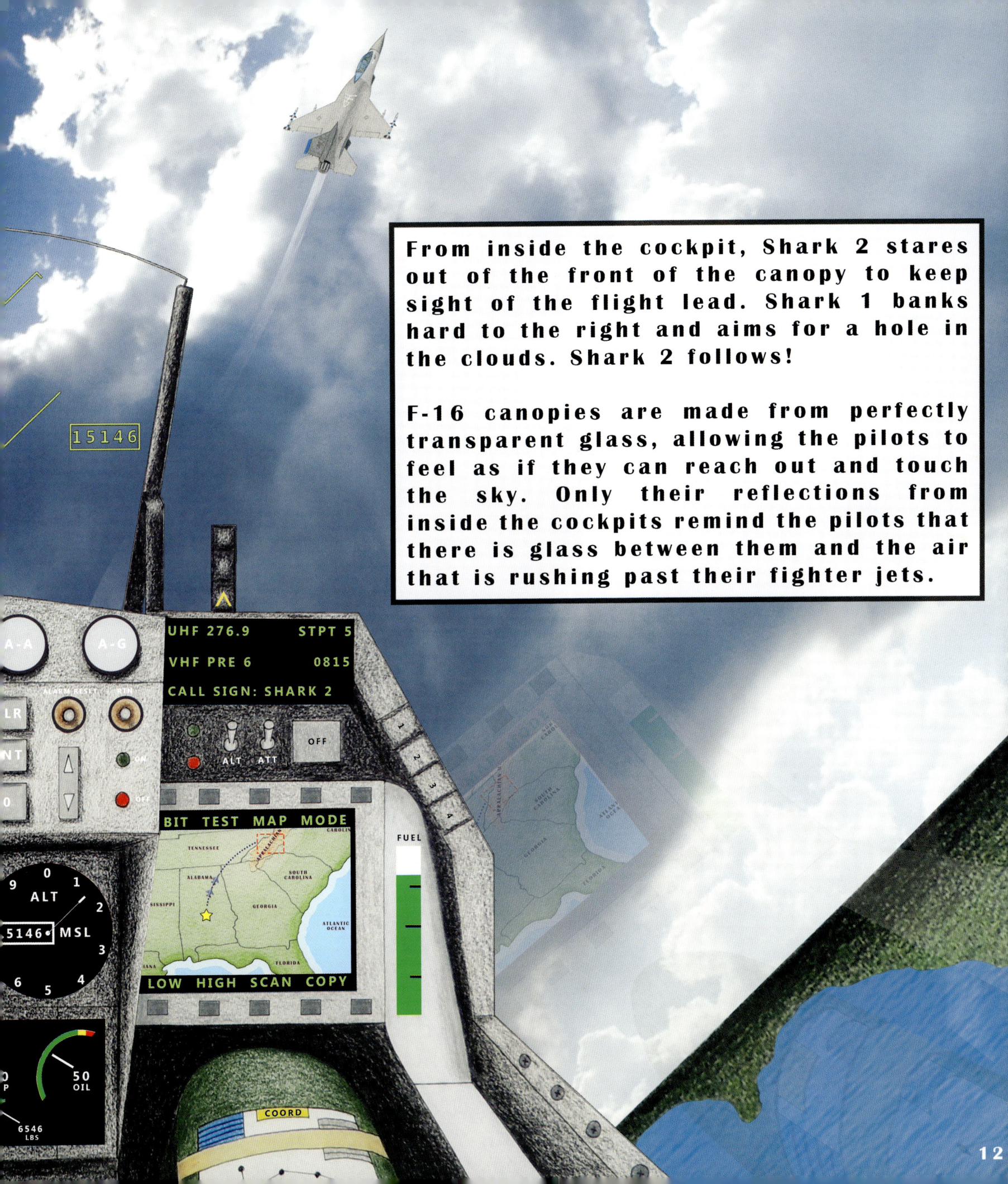

From inside the cockpit, Shark 2 stares out of the front of the canopy to keep sight of the flight lead. Shark 1 banks hard to the right and aims for a hole in the clouds. Shark 2 follows!

F-16 canopies are made from perfectly transparent glass, allowing the pilots to feel as if they can reach out and touch the sky. Only their reflections from inside the cockpits remind the pilots that there is glass between them and the air that is rushing past their fighter jets.

0845

Twenty thousand feet above earth's surface, traveling 500 miles per hour, the two jets in Shark Formation join up and race toward the military airspace. Once inside the invisible confines of the restricted area high above the mountains, these two Sharks will train by practice-fighting one another.

Today's fight will be a head-to-head matchup—an "old-school" dogfight with "new-school" planes. With the fight only minutes away, the pilots mentally review their game plans, which consist of various maneuvers, speeds, and the employment of simulated (fake) weapons in order to win both the aerial battle and bragging rights.

0902

"The fight is on!" Shark 1 yells over the radio. The formation of F-16s performs a high-speed pass that approaches the speed of sound, or 800 miles per hour! The combination of high speed and extreme maneuvering of the planes create intense "g-forces" that put pressure on the pilots' bodies, causing them to breathe heavily. Shark 2, straining to keep sight of Shark 1, looks out the back of the canopy and eagerly awaits the other pilot's first strategic maneuver.

In an instant, Shark 1 performs an inverted roll and descends toward the ground. Shark 2 follows suit, and the two jets brawl in a spiraling, downward fight. Whoever can jockey their fighter jet behind the other has the best chance to win, but who will that be? Only time will tell...

0915
The green mountains rapidly grow larger as the fighter jets continue their twirling descent. Shark 2 looks out the front of the canopy and finds Shark 1 within striking distance. Knowing this target opportunity will last for only a few seconds, Shark 2 quickly hammers down on the missile button, launching a simulated weapon. Instantly, Shark 1 reacts by shedding burning flares, defeating the incoming threat by distracting the air-to-air missile with extremely high temperatures.

This ends today's fight in a draw, with Shark 1 narrowly escaping defeat.

Breathing hard, but with a well-earned smile under the mask, Shark 1 says, "This isn't my first rodeo. Let's knock this fight off and go air refuel; my gas is getting low."

Shark 2 replies, "Same here. My fuel gauge just hit yellow. Let's go find that tanker!"

1015
Hundreds of miles traveled, yet only an hour later, the thirsty fighter jets arrive at their planned air-to-air refueling point over the beautiful, blue Atlantic Ocean. Desperately needing fuel to continue powering their monstrous engines, Shark Formation spots the KC-135, which is ready to fill their gas tanks. This "Stratotanker" has a wingspan of over 130 feet and can lug hundreds of thousands of pounds of fuel across the world.

Shark 1 and Shark 2 flip pre-refueling switches, and in seconds, their air refueling doors, located behind the jets' cockpits, are open. The fighter pilots will take turns carefully maneuvering their F-16s within inches of the atmospheric gas station's boom. Shark 1, as the flight lead, proceeds to air refuel first.

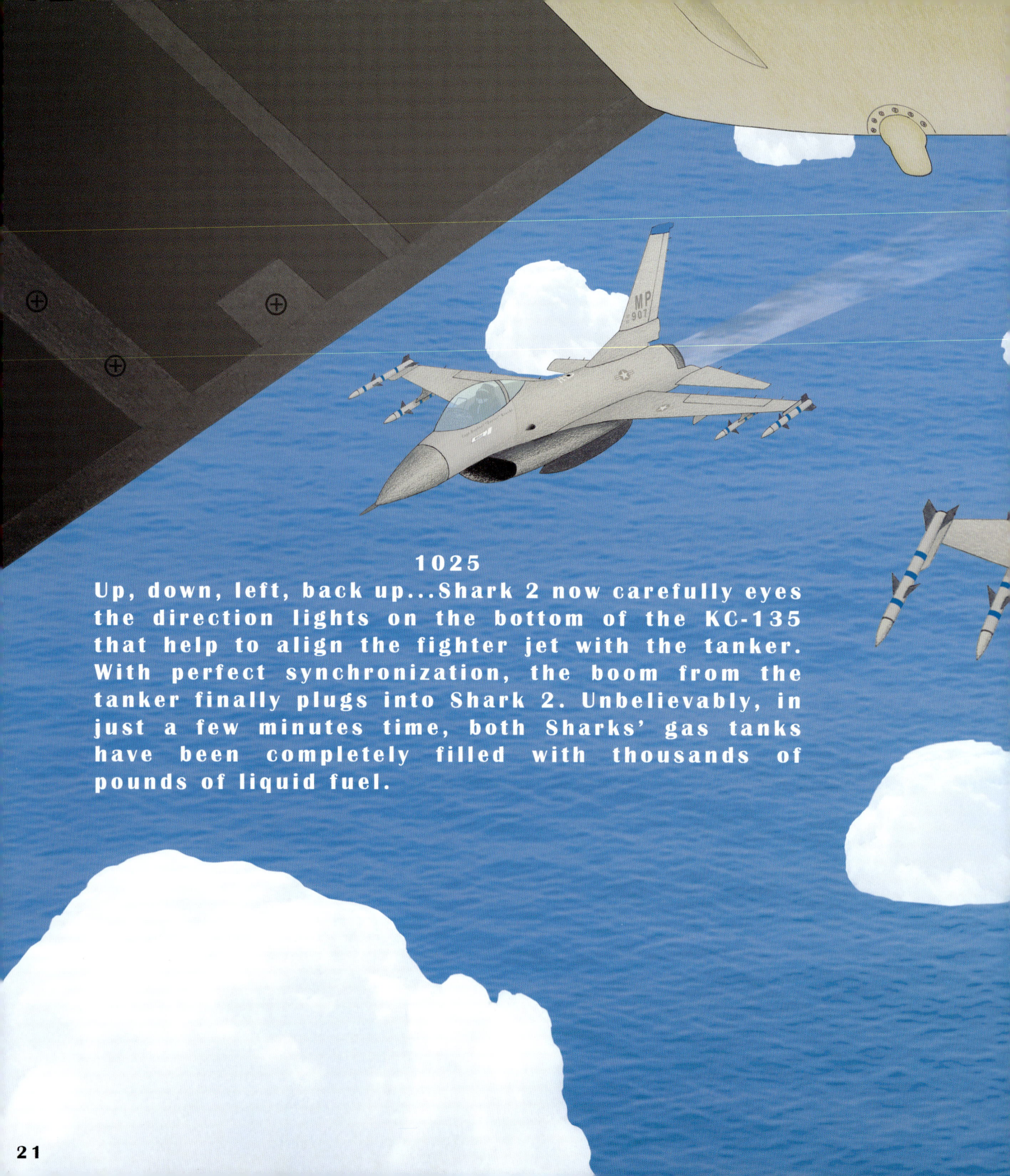

1025
Up, down, left, back up…Shark 2 now carefully eyes the direction lights on the bottom of the KC-135 that help to align the fighter jet with the tanker. With perfect synchronization, the boom from the tanker finally plugs into Shark 2. Unbelievably, in just a few minutes time, both Sharks' gas tanks have been completely filled with thousands of pounds of liquid fuel.

Over the radio, Shark 1 thanks the tanker crew for the fuel and directs Shark Formation to close their air refueling doors. "Shark 2, let's zoom to a higher altitude and speed on home!"

1130

The air is rare with less oxygen, and the blue sky begins to darken at 40,000 feet above sea level. The tails of the fighter jets scrape along the upper atmosphere as the pilots finally have a moment to breathe deeply and admire the curvature of the earth.

Up here, the world seems so small. Even the ride is smooth and peaceful.

Caution
Do Not Lift

Suddenly, muffled with static from one hundred miles away, home base control tower makes contact with the F-16s. "Shark Flight, welcome back! The wind has changed and is now out of the south. You are cleared to descend for final approach and landing on Runway 18."

Shark 1 radios Shark 2. "*Whew!* What a flight. Maybe next time you'll get me. I enjoyed flying with you, today. Unfortunately, it's time to head on down."

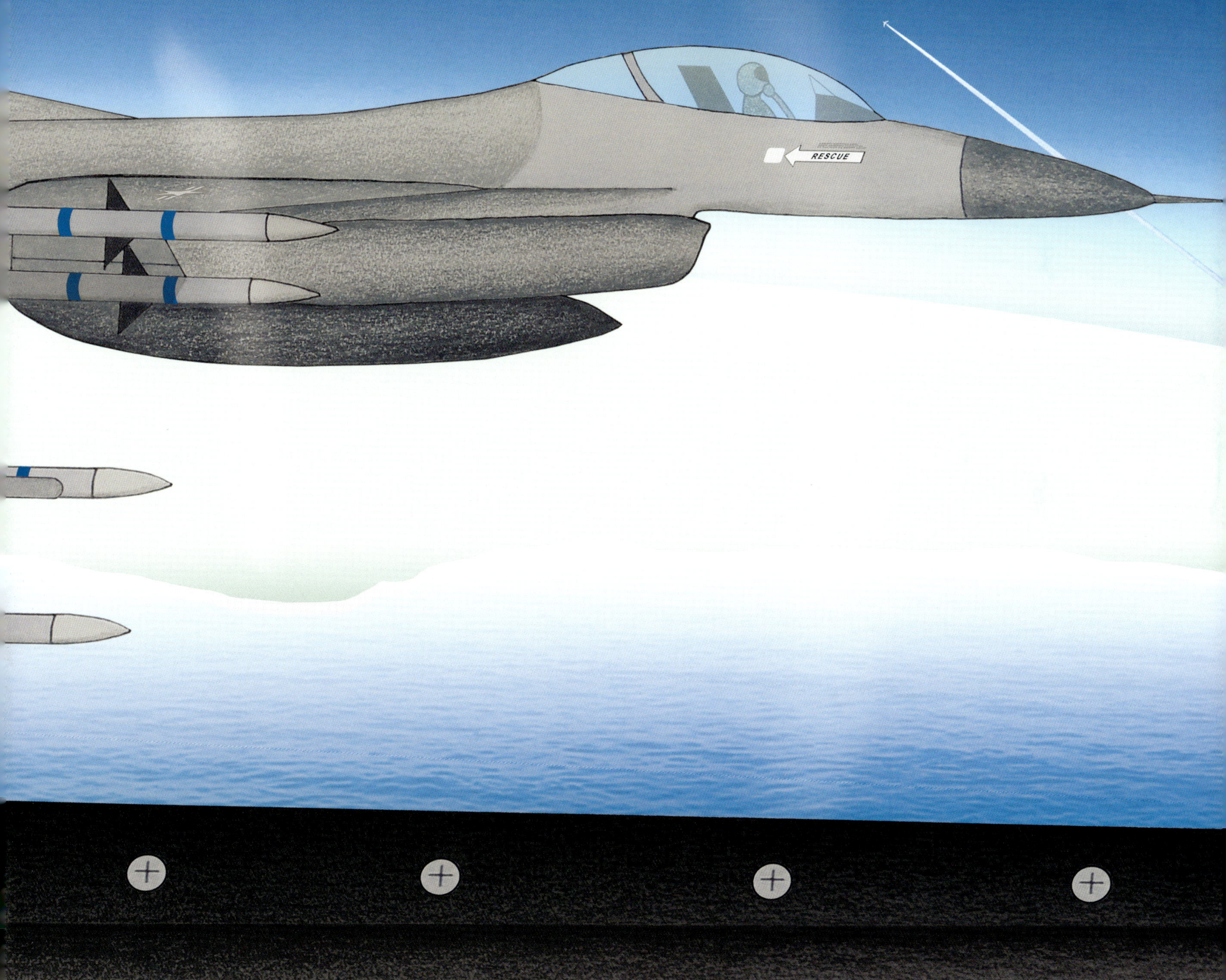

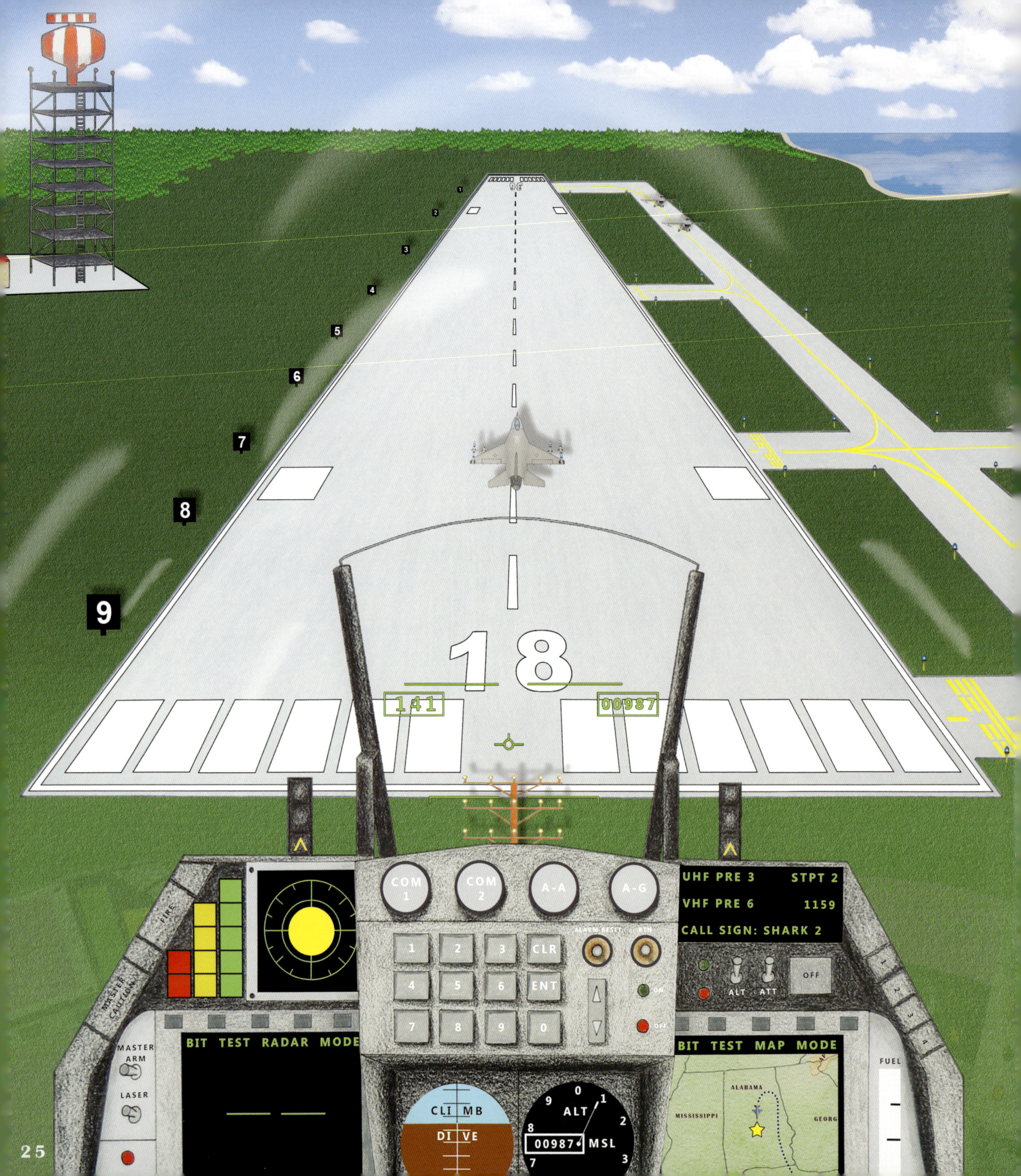

1159
Landing gear: *Down and locked.*
Aim point: *Set.*
Airspeed: *Perfect.*

Shark 2 watches out the front of the canopy as Shark 1 touches down on the runway. Then, Shark 2 receives permission from the control tower operator: "Shark 2, you are cleared to land on Runway 18."

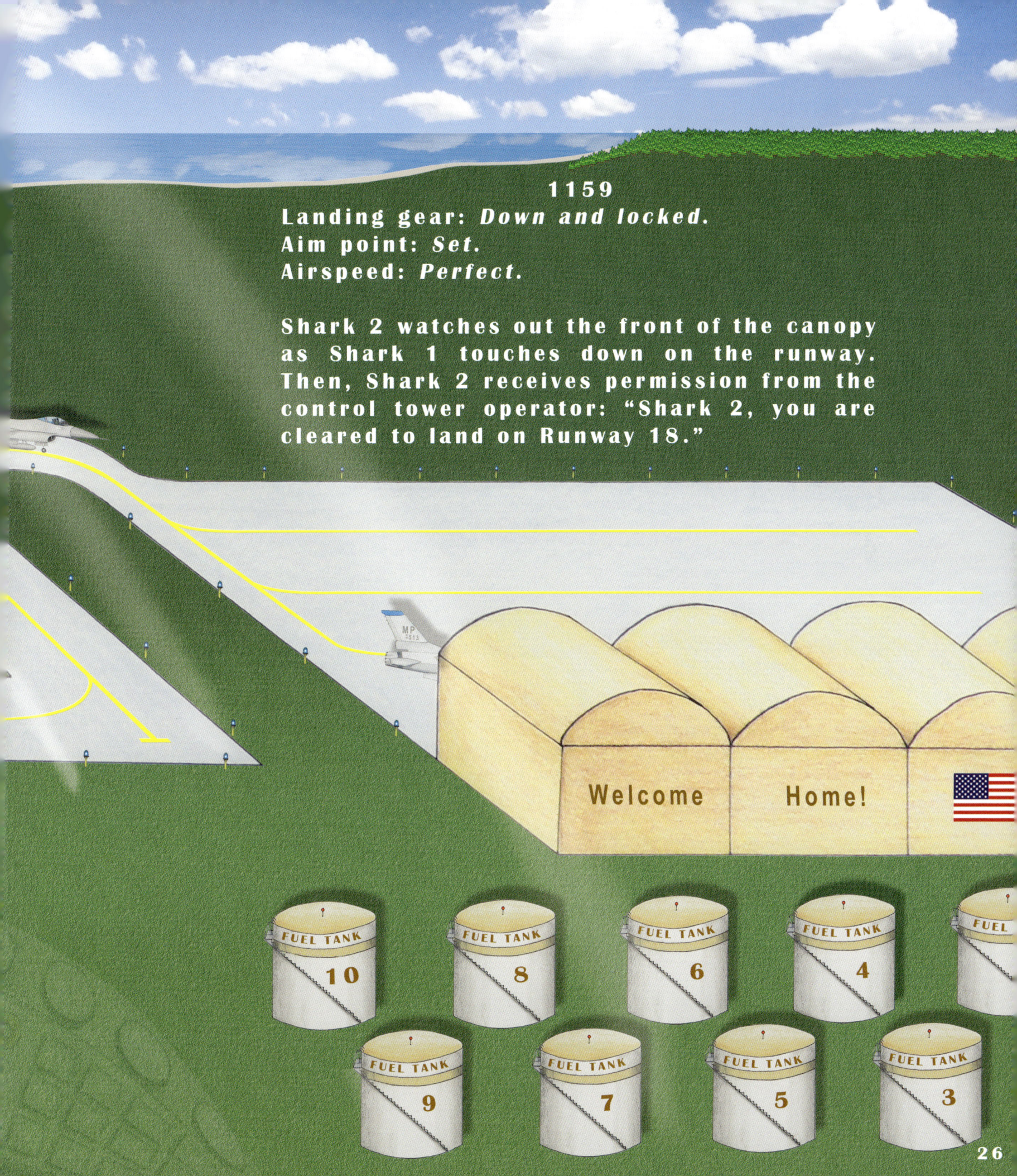

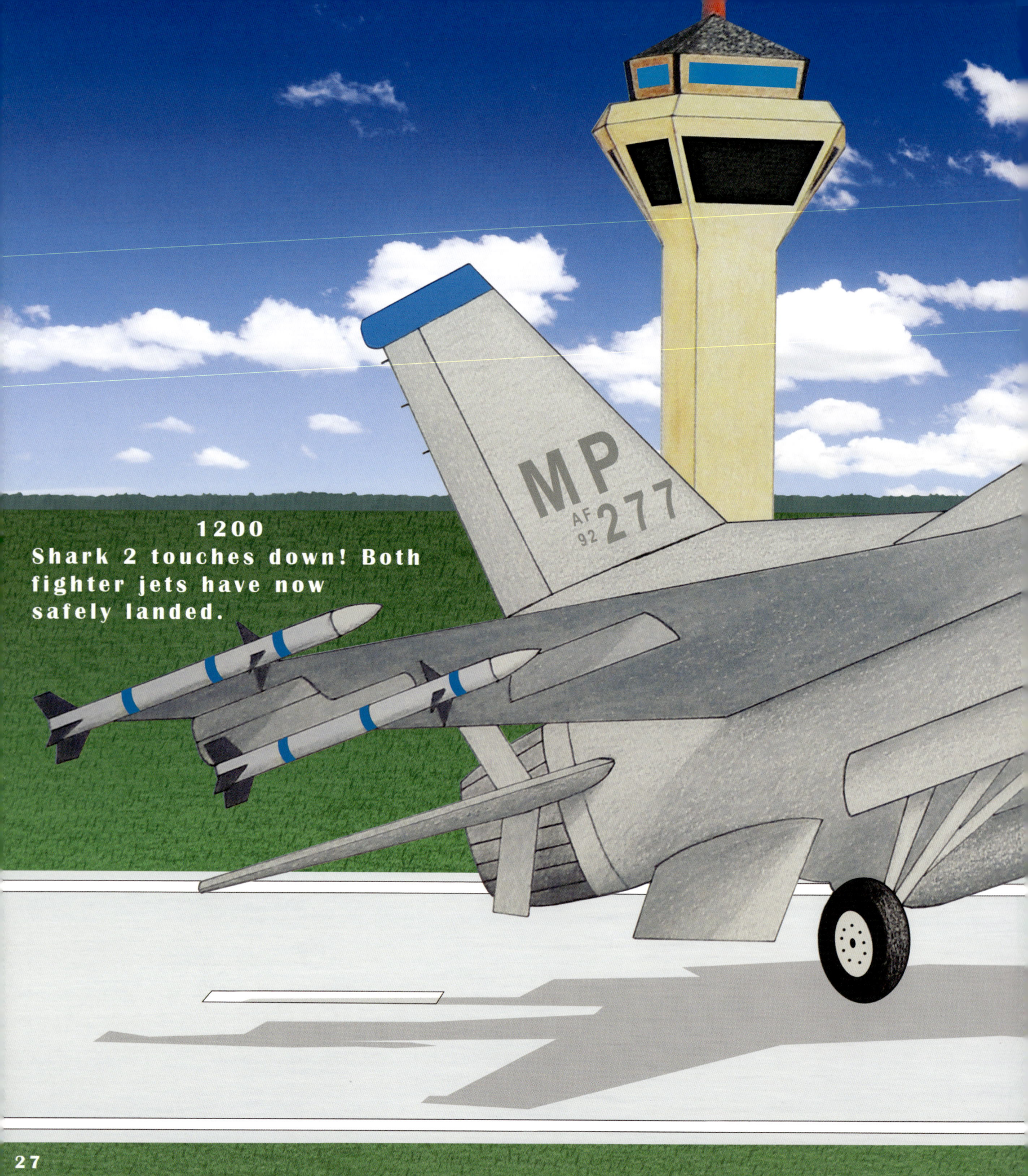

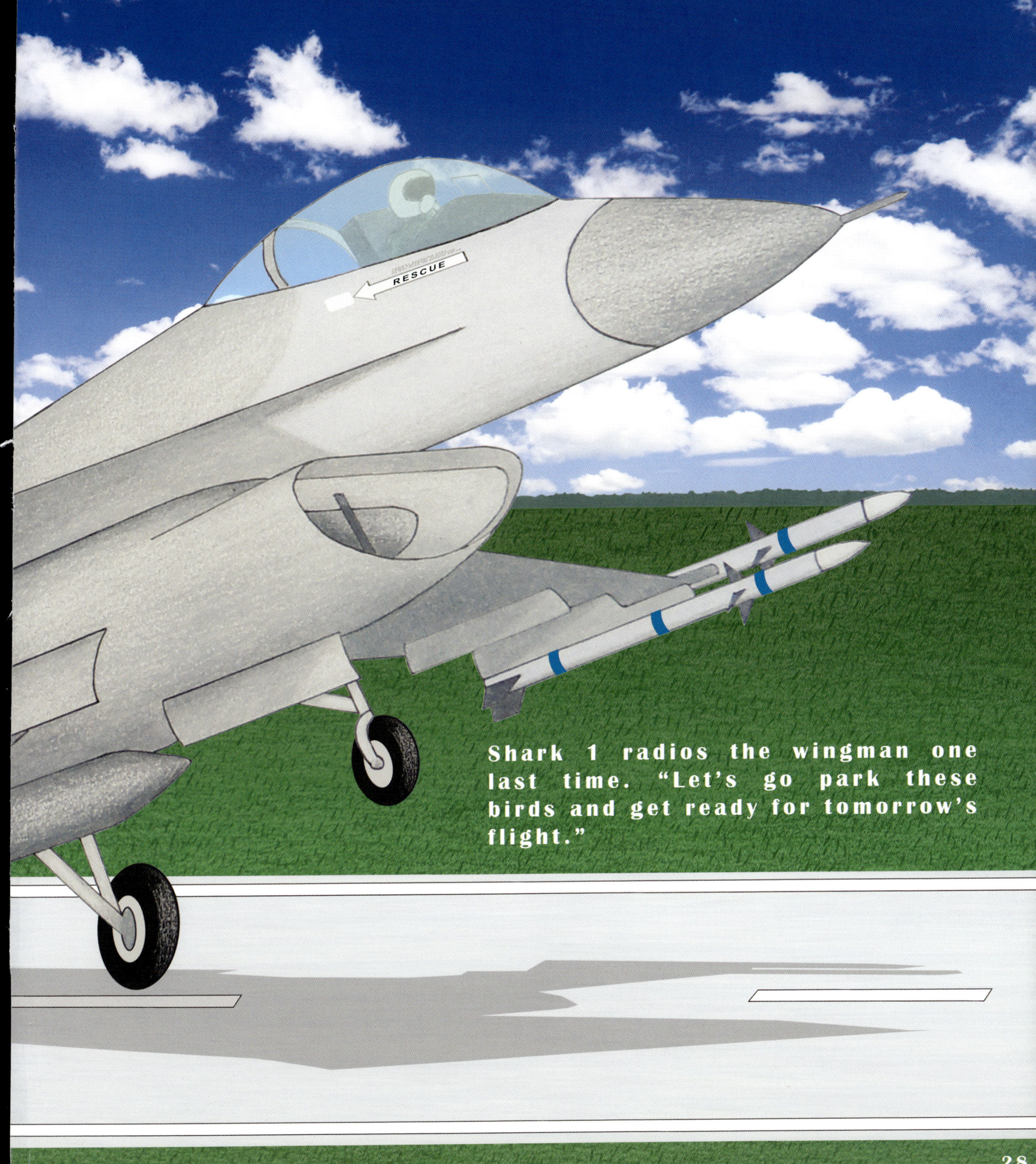

Shark 1 radios the wingman one last time. "Let's go park these birds and get ready for tomorrow's flight."

The End

MP
Majella Publishing

F-16

FRONT VIEW

13 FT

33 FT

TOP VIEW

9 FT

45 FT

SIDE VIEW

16 FT